Notes for Parents

Fairy stories have a very long history; so long that we do not know when and by whom they were first invented. That they continue to survive is proof of their popularity with children of many generations and cultures.

The stories selected for this series are particularly helpful to young listeners and readers. The constant, natural use of refrains with events often repeated, enable children to enjoy the security of repetition and the pleasure of anticipation. Familiarity with the various characters in the stories helps children to identify with them and work through their own feelings of kindness, consideration, aggression, fear and frustration. The expectation of good being rewarded and evil punished is rarely unsatisfied.

In these Usborne versions, the spirit of the original story has been retained and the simple text and sensitive illustrations bring a real freshness to these treasured tales.

Fairy stories will continue to fascinate children of a wide range of ages; read this lovely book together, often.

Betty Root

SLEEPING BEAUTY

Retold by Heather Amery
Illustrated by Stephen Cartwright

Language Consultant: Betty Root
There is a little yellow duck to find on every page.

TIGER BOOKS INTERNATIONAL

Once upon a time, there was a good and wise King and Queen. But they were always very sad because they had no children.

At long last, after waiting many years, a baby daughter was born. The King and Queen were delighted and loved the little Princess very much.

When the baby Princess was christened, the King and Queen gave a great feast at the Palace. Six good fairies came but the King had forgotten to invite the wicked, bad-tempered fairy whom no one had seen for years. When she heard about the feast, she was angry and thought up a wicked plan.

After the feast, the good fairies made wishes for the baby. When she grew up, they wanted her to be good, clever, beautiful and to sing and dance.

The sixth good fairy was just about to make her wish, when the wicked fairy appeared, looking very angry. She had come without being asked.

"This is my wish for the Princess," she said.
"When she is seventeen, she will prick her finger
on a spinning wheel. Then she will die."

"Oh, no," cried the sixth good fairy. "I can't
change that but my wish for her is that she won't
die, but will go to sleep for a hundred years."

The King shouted and the Queen cried but the wicked fairy disappeared in a puff of smoke.

"Well," said the King. "I'll make a new law. All the spinning wheels in my kingdom are to be burned at once. If there are no spinning wheels, then the Princess can't prick her finger on one."

As the years passed and the Princess grew up, she became good, clever and beautiful, and she could sing and dance.

On her seventeenth birthday, there was a Grand Ball at the Palace, and the six good fairies came. Everyone had forgotten all about the wicked fairy.

The next day, the Princess found a little staircase in the Palace that she had never seen before.

When she pushed open the door, she saw an old woman sitting at a spinning wheel.

"Come in, my dear," said the old woman, who was really the wicked fairy.

"What are you doing?" asked the Princess. She had never seen a spinning wheel before.

"I'm spinning," said the old woman. "I'll show you how to do it. Come and hold this."

The Princess put out her hand.

"Oh, I've pricked my finger," she said.

In a second, the Princess was fast asleep. Downstairs the King yawned, the Queen yawned and everyone else yawned. Then they went to sleep.

The wicked fairy disappeared and the six good fairies carried the sleeping Princess to her bedroom and laid her gently on her bed.

In the Palace, nothing, not even a mouse, moved for a hundred years. Outside, a thick forest grew up all around until only the roofs showed above the tree tops.

No one ever went near it except the good fairies, who watched over it while everyone slept.

After exactly one hundred years, a young Prince went hunting near the Palace. He saw the roofs above the trees and asked an old man about them.

"My Grandfather told me it's an enchanted Palace and there's a beautiful Princess asleep in there," said the old man. "But there's no way in."

The Prince thanked the old man and walked towards the Palace. But when he reached the trees they moved apart and let him through.

He ran up the Palace steps, past the sleeping guards and in through the open door. Nothing moved. It was so quiet, it was very creepy.

The Prince searched the whole Palace and, at last, came to the Princess's bedroom. When he saw her lying asleep, he thought she was so beautiful, he bent over and kissed her very gently. The Princess opened her eyes and smiled at him.

"You have come at last," she said.

All over the Palace, everyone woke up, yawned, stretched, shook off the dust and started to talk and move around.

"I'm hungry," said the King. "Tonight we'll have a great feast." He thanked the Prince for coming to their rescue and the Queen invited him to stay.

The next day, the Prince asked the King if he might marry the Princess.

"Of course," said the King, and the Princess said, "Yes, please."

Soon there was a very grand wedding and the Prince and Princess lived happily ever after.

First published in 1981 by Usborne Publishing Ltd, 83-85 Saffron Hill, London, EC1N 8RT, England. Copyright © 1992, 1988 Usborne Publishing Ltd.

This edition published in 1997 by Tiger Books International PLC, Twickenham. ISBN 1-85501-966-3